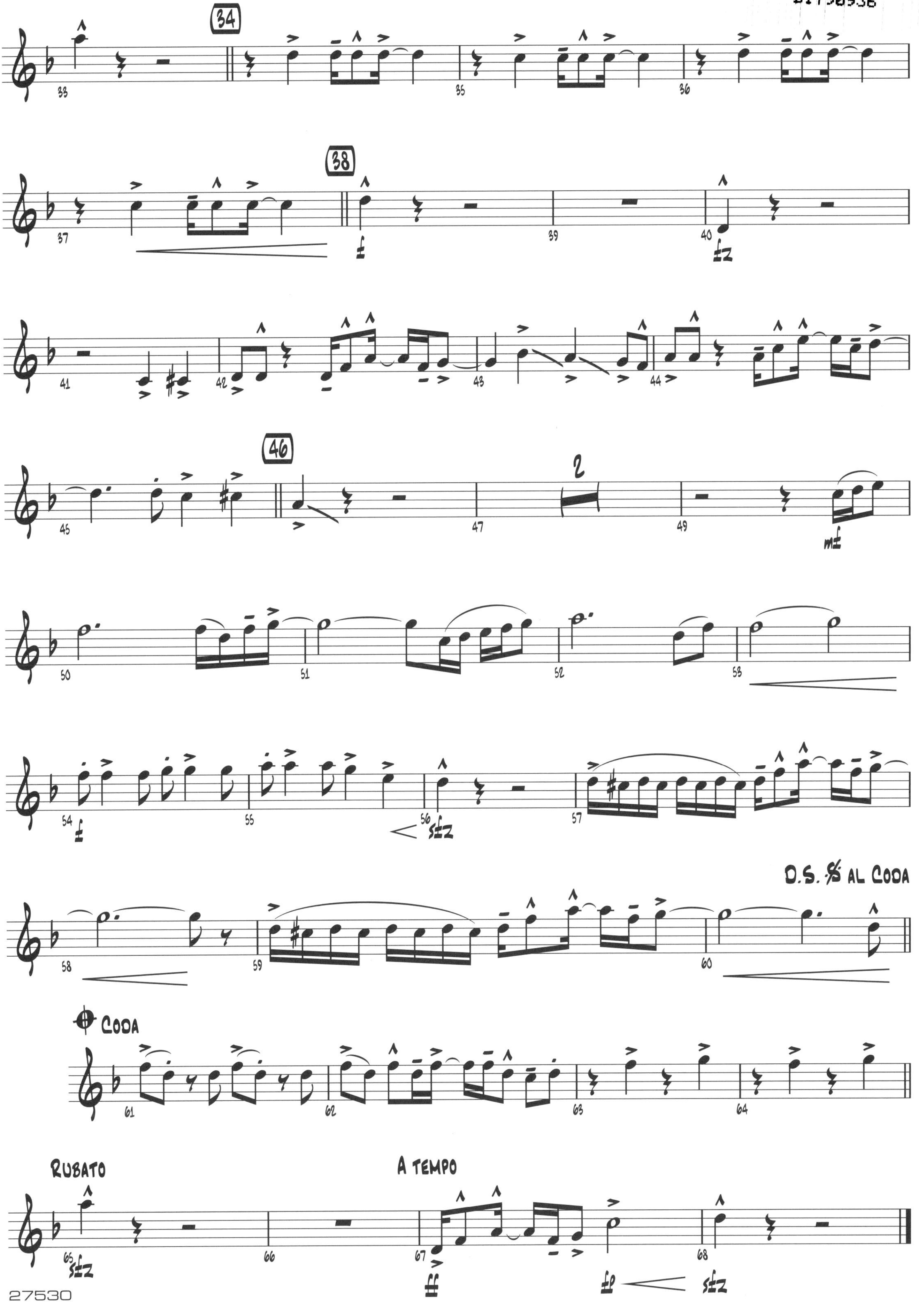
34
38
46
D.S. % al Coda
Coda
Rubato
A tempo

SITTIN' IN with the BIG BAND

B♭ Tenor Saxophone

jazz ensemble play-along

Track 1: tune to B♭ concert.

	Page #	Demo track	Play-Along track
Vehicle	2	2	3
Sax to the Max	4	4	5
Nutcracker Rock	6	6	7
Fiesta Latina	8	8	9
Now What	10	10	11
Goodbye My Heart	12	12	13
Two and a Half Men	14	14	15
Burritos to Go	16	16	17
Drummin' Man	18	18	19
Swingin' Shanty	20	20	21
Play That Funky Music	22	22	23
Performance Notes	24		

How to Use This Book

Each arrangement has two CD tracks:
1) Demonstration track. The Tenor Saxophone part is in the mix. Listen to how your part is played by professional musicians to copy the phrasing, intonation, articulation, feel, style, section/ensemble blend and concept.
2) Play-Along track. Your part has been taken out of the mix. You play-along with the big band.
3) See page 24 for Performance Notes
4) There is a two-measure count-off click at the beginning of each play-along track.

Alfred Publishing Co. Inc. thanks the students of
Mary Ward Catholic Secondary School Jazz Ensemble, Toronto, Canada,
John Volpe, director, Vince Gassi, assistant director, and photographers Jackie Fong and Jermaine Ong.

Alfred Publishing Co., Inc.
16320 Roscoe Blvd., Suite 100
P.O. Box 10003
Van Nuys, CA 91410-0003
alfred.com

A Division of ALFRED PUBLISHING CO., INC.
All Rights Reserved Including Public Performance

Any duplication, adaptation or arrangement of the compositions contained in this book requires the written consent of the Publisher.
No part of this book may be photocopied or reproduced in any way without permission.
Unauthorized uses are an infringement of the U.S. Copyright Act and are punishable by law.

ISBN-10: 0-7390-4514-8

5

NUTCRACKER ROCK

1st Bb Tenor Saxophone

By TCHAIKOWSKY
Arranged by MIKE SMUKAL

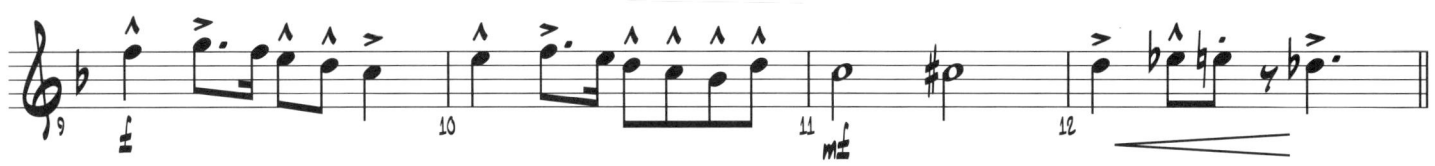

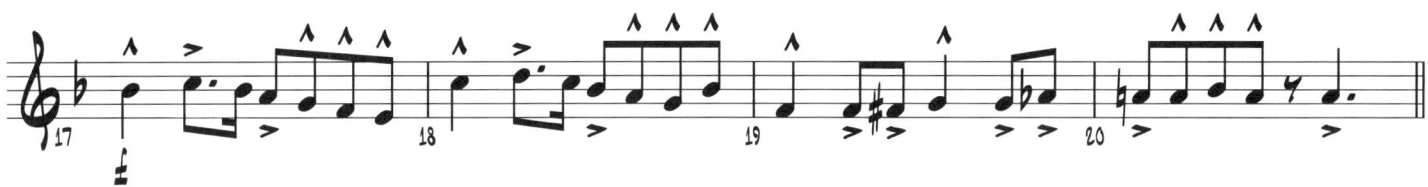

© 2006 Alfred Publishing Co., Inc.
All Rights Reserved

FIESTA LATINA

1st Bb Tenor Saxophone

VICTOR LOPEZ

NOW WHAT

By MIKE KAMUF

1st Bb Tenor Saxophone

GOODBYE MY HEART

By MIKE SMUKAL

1st Bb Tenor Saxophone

This page left blank to assist with page turns.

PERFORMANCE NOTES FOR TENOR SAX

Playing the 1st tenor sax chair in a big band is challenging but rewarding. Here are a few tips for playing tenor sax in a big band:
- Focus on blend, intonation, articulation, phrasing, and playing with accurate time. In addition, listen to the lead alto and match the style, pitch, sound, and feel.
- Don't over blow on the loud dynamics because it may affect your intonation.
- Listen for your part within the section harmony.
- In a rock or Latin style chart, the eighth notes are played even.
- In a rock style arrangement chart, carefully observe the rhythmic syncopation.
- Observe articulations and dynamic markings throughout the charts.
- Make sure you can hear the recording well (use headphones) so you can lock in your time and feel with the band.
- The marcato or rooftop accent (^) is played detached but not staccato, think "daht."
- Try recording yourself while you play along with the play-along track and see how close you can get to sounding like you are in the band
- Have fun being the "virtual" 1st tenor player!

There is a two-measure count-off click at the beginning of each play-along track

Vehicle:
1) In measure 8, listen carefully to the other saxes and play the unison section with accurate intonation.
2) Don't lay back—play with energy and forward motion.
3) The quarter notes in measures 31–32 and 63–64 are accented and long, think "dah."
4) In 66, the trombone plays rubato, and then the drumset plays a fill in-tempo to bring you in for the last two measures.

Sax to the Max:
1) Play the soli lines smoothly with an even sound.
2) Listen for your part in the section harmony. Blend!
3) The marcato or rooftop accent (^) is played detached.
4) Play the last eighth note in a group short.

Nutcracker Rock:
1) In this rock/march style, play the eighth notes even.
2) The marcato or rooftop accent (^) is played detached.
3) In measure 41, play the unison line with the trumpet as one—listen!
4) Accurate articulation is critical in this arrangement.

Fiesta Latina:
1) This Latin style chart has plenty of unison lines therefore good air support is critical to maintain accurate intonation. Listen and blend!
2) At measure 53, listen and match the articulation with the other instruments.
3) Measure 65 is a solo. Play as written or ad lib. The Ami and G chords both use the notes in the G major scale.

Now What:
1) Listen carefully in the unison lines with the alto and trumpets.
2) Observe the articulation.

Goodbye My Heart:
1) For this ballad, use plenty of air for good support which will help intonation and phrasing.
2) Even though the dynamic level is soft, play with a full sound and avoid pinching the embouchure and tone. Listen and blend.
3) Ballads look easy but require concentration.

Two and a Half Men:
1) Listen and blend in the unison section at measure 17.
2) Beginning in measure 13, the "and" of beat 4 is played short for this repeated lick. The tied note is not actually played. This is common notation in jazz music.
3) The solo can be played as written or ad lib in the style of the chart.

Burritos to Go:
1) Play the marcato accents (^) detached but not staccato.
2) The last eighth note in a group is short.
3) Play the solo as written or ad lib. Learn the notes in the chords and look for common notes in the different chords to help you navigate through the chord progression.

Drummin' Man:
1) This traditional swing style is concise and tight. Listen and match the articulation.
2) The last eighth note in a group is short.
3) Listen for your part within the section harmony.

Swingin' Shanty:
1) Play the eighths with a strong swing feel.
2) Play the backgrounds second time at measure 51.
3) Play the triplets with accurate time.
4) At measure 71, play in unison with the trombones and bass. Match the articulation and phrasing.

Play That Funky Music:
1) Observe the accents and articulation. Listen!
2) Play the two sixteenth notes with a "doo-dit" articulation.

Recorded at **Bias Recording Studios,** Springfield, VA
Bob Dawson, Engineer
Featuring the **Belwin Jazz Big Band, Pete BarenBregge,** Director.

Learn **jazz concepts, improvisation** and **sight reading** for all instruments from jazz legend **Bob Mintzer!**

Play Along Book & CDs

- 12 jazz etudes composed by Bob Mintzer in a variety of jazz styles, tempos, and time signatures
- Performance notes/tips for each etude to assist in interpretation and improvisation
- Play-along CD with a stellar rhythm section
- All books are compatible and written so they can be performed together!

12 Contemporary Jazz Etudes Book & CD

(ELM04011)	C Instruments—Flute, Guitar, Violin, Keyboards	$24.95
(ELM04012)	B♭ Tenor Saxophone and Soprano Saxophone	$24.95
(ELM04013)	E♭ Instruments—Alto and Baritone Saxophone	$24.95
(ELM04014)	B♭ Trumpet and Clarinet	$24.95
(ELM04015)	Bass Clef Instruments—Trombone, Baritone, Horn and Tuba	$24.95

also available from Bob Mintzer and Belwin Jazz:

The Music of Bob Mintzer: Solo Transcriptions and Performing Artist Master Class CD
Book & CD

(0479B) $24.95

15 Easy Jazz, Blues & Funk Etudes
Book & CD

(ELM00029CD)	C Instruments—Flute, Guitar Keyboards	$19.95
(ELM00030CD)	B♭ Instruments Tenor Saxophone and Soprano Saxophone	$19.95
(ELM00031CD)	E♭ Instruments—Alto and Baritone Saxophone	$19.95
(ELM00033CD)	B♭ Trumpet and Clarinet	$19.95
(ELM00032CD)	Bass Clef Instruments—Trombone, Baritone, Horn and Tuba	$19.95

14 Blues & Funk Etudes
Book & CD

(EL9604CD)	C Instruments—Flute, Guitar Keyboards	$26.95
(EL9605CD)	B♭ Instruments Tenor Saxophone and Soprano Saxophone	$26.95
(EL9607CD)	E♭ Instruments—Alto and Baritone Saxophone	$26.95
(EL9606CD)	B♭ Trumpet	$26.95
(EL9608CD)	Bass Clef Instruments—Trombone, Baritone, Horn and Tuba	$26.95

14 Jazz & Funk Etudes
Book & CD

(EL03949)	C Instruments—Flute, Guitar Keyboards	$24.95
(EL03950)	B♭ Instruments Tenor Saxophone and Soprano Saxophone	$24.95
(EL03952)	E♭ Instruments—Alto and Baritone Saxophone	$24.95
(EL03951)	B♭ Trumpet	$24.95
(EL03953)	Bass Clef Instruments—Trombone, Baritone, Horn and Tuba	$24.95

Belwin JAZZ
a division of **Alfred**

All prices in US Dollars and subject to change.
wo 53816

ORDER MUSIC TODAY
Learn what you need, play what you want.
OrderMusicToday.com

Jazz up your theory skills with
Alfred's Essentials of JAZZ THEORY

Written by renowned jazz educator and former IAJE President, Shelly Berg, this course is designed for students who have successfully completed one year of traditional music theory, or who are already familiar with basic theory concepts such as those taught in Books 1–3 of *Alfred's Essentials of Music Theory*.

Ideal for jazz enthusiasts & students alike!

Book 1 includes: Basic Elements (Melody, Harmony, Rhythm, Texture, Form) • Swing Feel, Swing Eighth Notes, Swing Groove • Syncopation, Bebop Style, Lick, Line & Melodic Soloing • Major Triad, Major Scale, Consonance • Major Seventh Chords, Chord Changes • Tonic Function, Scalar Melody, Passing & Neighboring Tones • Dissonant 4th and Resolution • Subdominant Major Seventh Chords, Voice Leading for Tonic & Subdominant Major Seventh Chords • Modes, Lydian Scale • Hierarchy of 3rd & 7th • Major 9th Chords, Major 6/9 Chords, Major Pentatonic Scale • Grace Notes, Scoops & Turns • Dominant 7th and 9th Chords, Dominant Function • Resolution of V7 Chords, Tendency Tones and Tritone • V7–I MA7 Common Tones and Voice Leading • Dominant Scale (Mixolydian), Bebop Dominant Scale • "Bluesy" Dominant Chords, Blue Notes, 12-Bar Blues Progression, Blues Scale • Glossary & Index of Terms & Symbols

Book 2 includes: Counterpoint-Bass and Melody • Walking Bass Lines • Walking Bass Lines in the Circle of Fifths, Two-Note Voicings • Comping & Comp Rhythms, Voice Leading • Brazilian Bass Lines & Comping Patterns • Minor 7th and 9th Chords & Inversions • Supertonic Function–$iimi^7$ and $iimi^9$ Chords • Resolution of $iimi^7$ to V7 • The ii-V-I Turnaround Progression • Jazz Language—Combined Scale / Arpeggio & "The ii-V Lick" • Jazz Language—Triplet Arpeggio & "The Bebop Dominant Lick"—Dominant 13th Chords & ii-V-I Voicings • Passing Minor +7 Chord & Progression • Tonicisation of the IV Chord • The ii-V Turnaround to IV • Melody for the Turnaround to IV • II Dominant Seventh Chords • ii^7 (#11) Chords, Lydian Dominant Scale, I Augmented Chord Extension (I+) • Diminished 7th Chords & Diminished Scales • Diminished 7th Function & Melodic Language • VI7 ($\flat$9) Chord, The Turnback Progression • AABA Standard Song Form—"Take the A-Train" Progression • Jazz Language—Chromatic Leading Tones, Bebop Scales • Jazz Language—Auxiliary "Enclosure" Tones • The Jazz Blues Progression, Finding the Chromatics • Glossary & Index of Terms & Symbols.

Book 3 includes: Jazz Language—Melodic, Soloing & Melodic Sequence • Afro-Cuban Jazz—Clave & Tumbau • Afro-Cuban Jazz—Cascara & Montuno • Drop-Two Voicings • Minor 11th Chords & Sus Chords • Minor Tonic Chord, Jazz Minor Scale • Minor ii-V Turnaround, Half-Diminished Chord & V7 Chord • Resolutions and Voice Leading • Jazz Language—Scales for the Half-Diminished Chord • Jazz Language—Harmonic-Minor Scale & Lick for V7($\flat$9) • Turnaround to iv in Minor Keys • Minor Turnback, VI7-VI7($\flat$9)-i Cadence • Blues Scale in Minor Keys, Minor Pentatonic & Pentatonic / Blues Scales • Turnarounds to III, VI and VII in Minor Keys • Minor 12-bar Blues Progression • Minor Turnarounds in Major Keys–to ii and vi • Minor Turnaround in Major Keys–to iii, Deceptive Cadence (Backdoor Cadence) • Altered Dominant Chords • Jazz Language—Diminished Scale for Dominant Chords & Altered Dominant Cell • Jazz Language—Altered Dominant Lick and Scale • Step-Down Progression • IV-I (Plagal) Progressions, Backdoor Progressions • I-VI Progressions • ABAC Standard Song Form • Slash Chords • Glossary & Index of Terms & Symbols.

(00-20806)	Alfred's Essentials of Jazz Theory Book 1 & CD	$12.95
(00-20808)	Alfred's Essentials of Jazz Theory Book 2 & CD	$12.95
(00-20810)	Alfred's Essentials of Jazz Theory Book 3 & CD	$12.95
(00-20812)	Alfred's Essentials of Jazz Theory Complete (Books 1–3) & 3 CDs	$34.95
(00-22008)	Alfred's Essentials of Jazz Theory Teacher's Answer Key w/ 3 CDs	$37.50

Alfred Publishing Co., Inc.
P.O. Box 10003 • Van Nuys, CA 91419-0003
customerservice@alfred.com

Conquer theory fears with Alfred's
ESSENTIALS OF MUSIC THEORY

By Andrew Surmani, Karen Farnum Surmani, Morton Manus

The most complete music theory course ever!

This all-in-one series includes concise lessons with short exercises, ear-training activities and reviews. Available in three separate volumes or as a complete set, *Essentials of Music Theory* also includes Ear-Training CDs (performed by acoustic instruments), a Teacher's Answer Key Book, reproducible Teacher's Activity Kits, Bingo Games, Flash Cards and Computer Software. The Alto Clef edition includes primarily alto clef examples, with some treble and bass clef examples as well.

	Volume 1	Volume 2	Volume 3	Complete
BOOKS				
Student Book	(00-17231) $6.50	(00-17232) $6.50	(00-17233) $6.50	(00-17234) $12.50
Student Book w/2 Ear-Training CDs	—	—	—	(00-16486) $31.50
Student Book / Alto Clef (Viola) Edition	(00-18580) $6.50	(00-18581) $6.50	(00-18582) $6.50	(00-18583) $19.95
NEW! Student Book / Alto Clef w/2 Ear-Training CDs	—	—	—	(00-27642) $34.95
Teacher's Answer Key Book	—	—	—	(00-17256) $19.50
Teacher's Answer Key Book & 2 Ear-Training CDs	—	—	—	(00-17261) $37.50
EAR-TRAINING CDS				
Ear-Training CD		(00-17252) $10.95	(00-17253) $10.95	(00-17254) $18.95
DOUBLE BINGO GAMES				
NEW! Key Signature Double Bingo	—	—	—	(00-24448) $19.95
Note Naming Double Bingo	—	—	—	(00-19481) $19.95
Rhythm Double Bingo	—	—	—	(00-19479) $19.95
FLASH CARDS				
NEW! Key Signature Flash Cards	—	—	—	(00-24447) $9.95
Note Naming Flash Cards	—	—	—	(00-20320) $9.95
Rhythm Flash Cards	—	—	—	(00-19396) $9.95
TEACHER'S ACTIVITY KITS				
Teacher's Activity Kit	(00-19380) $19.95	(00-20373) $19.95	**NEW!** (00-26321) $19.95	**NEW!** (00-26327) $49.95
VERSION 2.0 SOFTWARE				
Student Version	(00-18827) $29.95	(00-20822) $39.95		(00-18833) $59.95
Educator Version	(00-18826) $99.95	(00-20821) $119.95		(00-18832) $199.95
Network Version (for 5 simultaneous users•)	(00-20322) $300.00	(00-20823) $350.00		(00-20321) $500.00

Which version do I need?

Student Version
- Ideal for individual students using the program one at a time
- Not necessary to track other users' progress

Educator Version
- Ideal for educators with one computer in a classroom, or for private lesson/studio use
- Educator has ability to track all users' progress & create custom tests

Network Version
- Includes all Educator Version features
- Designed for use on networked computers

•Additional Network User Licenses can be purchased as follows: **Volume 1**–$20 each, **Volumes 2 & 3**–$25 each, **Complete**–$40 each

Visit **alfred.com** and click on "Theory & Reference" for a handy interactive guide to help you decide which version is right for you.